Speedsters...

Desperate for a Dog

by Rose Impey
and Jolyne Knox

E. P. DUTTON   NEW YORK

for Rachel and Holly

Speedsters is a trademark of Dutton Children's Books.

Text copyright © 1988 by Rose Impey
Illustrations copyright © 1988 by Jolyne Knox

Library of Congress Cataloging-in-Publication Data

Impey, Rose.
  Desperate for a dog/by Rose Impey; illustrated by Jolyne Knox.
—1st ed.
    p.   cm.
  Summary: Two sisters who are desperate to get a dog meet with
firm opposition from their father, until their family is asked
to take care of a sick neighbor's dog for several weeks.
  ISBN 0-525-44513-7
  [1. Dogs—Fiction.] I. Knox, Jolyne, ill. II. Title.
PZ7.I344De   1989   89-1239
[Fic]—dc19   CIP
                                                             AC

First published in the United States in 1989
by E. P. Dutton, a division of Penguin Books USA Inc.

Originally published in Great Britain
by A & C Black (Publishers) Ltd
35 Bedford Row, London WC1R 4JH

Printed in the U.S.A.
First Edition   10 9 8 7 6 5 4 3 2 1

Round One

My sister and I were desperate for a dog.
All our friends had dogs.
Our cousin had a cat
and a rabbit
and a dog.

Almost everyone on our street had dogs.

Everyone except us.
We just *had* to have one.

First we asked our dad.
"Dad, can we have a dog?
Please?"

He said,
"A dog? Oh no! No way."
And he started
to laugh.
"But why?" we said.
"Why can't we?"

So Dad put down his saw
and told us.
He gave us all sorts of reasons.

He counted them off on his fingers.
Against a dog:

1. Dogs make a mess.

We'd clean it up.

2. Dogs are noisy.

We'd keep it quiet.

3. Dogs need lots of exercise.

We'd walk it.

"And number seven," said Dad. "Who
would look after it while you two
are at school?

Me, of course.

I'd be the one at home with it."

And I don't even like dogs.

5

Well, that was true.
He is the one at home all day.
Our dad is unemployed.
He doesn't go out to work.
He's always busy making things,
in his workshop—
shelves and cupboards mostly.

Our house is full of cupboards.
But it's not the same.
He'd rather go to work.

"A dog would be company for you,"
I said, "when you're on your own
all day."

You could talk to it.

"A dog could be useful," I said.
"You could teach it things."
"Tricks," my sister said.
"To fetch your tools," I said.
"A dog can hold things in its mouth,"
my sister said. And then she got
carried away.

"I bet you could teach a smart dog
to saw wood,

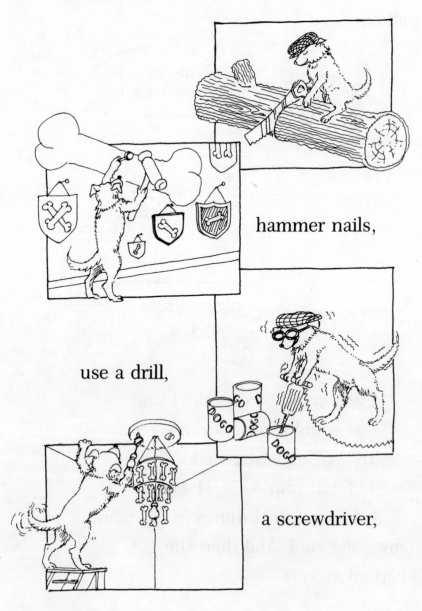

hammer nails,

use a drill,

a screwdriver,

8

a paintbrush,

hang wallpaper.

If it was really smart I bet it could
make its own doghouse!"

Sometimes my sister is pretty
stupid.

Dad started to laugh.
"I suppose we'd call it
Do-It-Yourself Dog," he said.
Then he laughed even harder.
Our dad always laughs most
at his own jokes.

"Come on," I said. "We'll go
ask Mom."

Mom was in the
spare bedroom—
wallpapering.

Please?

"Mom," we said,
"can we get a dog?"

"You don't want a dog," she said.
"You have a pet already."
Well, that was true. We did.

But you can't take a hamster
for a walk on a leash, can you?

"It's not the same," we said.
"We want a dog."
"More than anything in the whole
wide world," said my sister.

And her bottom lip trembled.

Mom put the paste brush in the bucket.
She sat down for a break.

"Tell me why," she said.
So we told her.
We tried to think of lots of reasons.
We started to count them on our fingers.

For a dog:

1. Dogs guard your house when you're out.

2. You can take dogs for walks.

3. Dogs are nice. You can have fun with them.

4. Um... um...

14

We couldn't seem to think of
any more.
So in the end we said,

WE JUST
WANT ONE!

Please, Mom?

Please!

"Well," said Mom,
"you'll have to ask
Dad. He's the one
at home all day.
It isn't really up to me."

Then Dad came in.
We smiled at him.
"Dad . . ."

Don't ask!
I've told you once.
The answer is no.
N...O... No.

No way.
Out of the question.
Absolutely ...no...no...
no...no...no...
no....
NO!

You could tell he meant it.
My sister burst out crying.

End of Round One.

Round Two

A few weeks later, just before my
sister's birthday, we went to stay
with Grandma and Grandpa.
We went in the car.
The ride went really quickly.

My sister and I made up
a new game.
We called it Spot the Dog.

As Mom drove along, we looked out
of the car windows.
We made a list of how many dogs
we saw, what kind they were
and what color.
Then we pretended they were our
dogs, and we chose names for them.

1. Queeny, a brown labrador
2. Benjie, a black spaniel
3. Coco, a brown sausage dog
4. Capt. Hook, a white sheepdog
5. Ice cream Sundae, a brown and white mongrel

LH 850D

The rule was that we could only count
dogs on our own side of the road.
It's hard writing in a car, especially when
you go around corners.

"Dad," I said, "how do you spell
shredded wheat?"

"You're going to call a dog
Shredded Wheat?" asked Dad.

"That airedale
over there.
It's just
like shredded wheat,
light brown and
crunchy," I said.

20

"It's not crunchy when the milk's on it," said my sister.
"It's all sloppy like a bowl of . . ."

"That's enough," said Mom. "We've heard that before."

"It is, though, isn't it?" said Dad, thinking about it.

"Oh, don't start her off," said Mom. "Just spell *shredded wheat,* will you."

My sister can hardly spell anything.
She did little drawings instead.

By the time we turned onto Grandma's
street, I'd counted eight dogs.
My sister had six.

We started to argue about one that
crossed from her side to mine.
Mom had to slow down to miss it.

"Can't you two talk about anything else?" said Mom. "You've got dogs on the brain."

"But that's *my* dog," I said.

"If it keeps on walking out in front of cars," said Dad, "it'll soon be a dead dog."

"That's not funny," I said.

"Horrible," said my sister.

In the end we both counted it.

When we looked up we were already there.

Grandma and Grandpa were standing at the fence.

After dinner, when we were ready
for bed, Grandpa said to my sister, "Well,
little cough drop, have you decided
what you want for your birthday?"

Grandpa always calls us funny names.
Mom and Dad say he spoils us.
I think he spoils my sister more.

My sister said, "It's a secret.
I want to whisper." And she climbed
onto his knee. She whispered
in his ear.

Grandpa began to smile.
"Is that all?" he said.
She just nodded.

"What's going on?" said Dad.
But my sister said, "It's private."

On her birthday my sister got lots
of presents.

All

shapes

From
Grandpa

and

Sizes

Grandpa's was the smallest.
She left it till the very last.
When she opened it her face turned
bright pink.

It was a collar and leash.

"But we don't even have a dog," I said.

"Not yet, we don't," she said.

Because it was her birthday,

Dad didn't say anything.

My sister started grinning.

End of Round Two.

Round Three

Every Saturday we get the local paper.
It comes about five o'clock.
Dad likes to look at it first,
to read the sports page.

Mom likes to see what's playing
at the movies and if there's anyone
she knows in the local news.
She takes forever to read it.
She works in a library.

She reads lots of books,
but she must be a slow reader.

"Can't you hurry up, Mom?" we said.
"We want to read the paper."

"You do?" said Mom. "What for?"
"The want ads," we said.
"You are a funny pair," she said.
But she handed it over.

Then my sister and I
sat together on the sofa.
We each held one
side of the paper.
We turned towards
the back.
At the top of the page
was an enormous word.
I couldn't read it.

"Miscellaneous Sales," said Mom.

There were long lists of things people were trying to sell: cement mixers and strollers and greenhouses and secondhand fur coats and video players. But the last row said, PET CORNER.

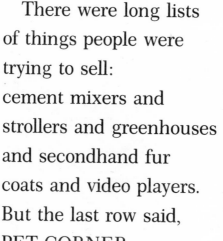

Here it is.

I began to read them out to my sister.
We circled the best ones
with black felt pen.

PET CORNER

Free to a good home, Labrador dog 4 years. Tel. 6827085

Persian Kittens, ready now. Tel. 9156771

Parrot Boarding. Good care and attention. Treated as own pets. All types of birds at fair prices. Tel. 2389716

Collie Puppies, ready now or wait till Christmas. Tel. 6032241

Pick of the litter — Great Dane puppies, blues, blacks and harlequins. Real dog lovers only. Tel. 7277703

THE DOG HOUSE Boarding Kennels

Many satisfied Clients. Call— Tel. 5656427

Jack Russell pups - very small, $25. also nice pony Tel. 7016981

Good homes for tabby kittens Twelve weeks. Tel. 4950617

Kitty Litter — 10 lb bags delivered to your door. Call now. Tel. 8960534

Double buggy, stair gate, 4 chairs, tropical fish and sandwich-maker. Tel. 3654213

As new - Dropside Cot. Cosytoes, Kiddie Carrier, Camping Cot and Baby Nest. Tel. 5182612

SHEDS call Tel.

General

For sale. 3-man tent, sandbox with cover and a very large houseplant. Tel. 2356785

Tortoise Help Line- Any problems and advice. Call 3724447

"For goodness sake," said Dad. "You
sound like a pair of pigeons. Now
stop reading those stupid ads
and come to dinner."

At bedtime my sister and I took the paper upstairs with us. Instead of a bedtime story, I read her the ads.

Last of the litter
Sheltie puppy (female)
– must find home
soon.
Looking for someone
to love her.
Tel. 696 4871
6—10 pm.

When I'd finished she said, "Read me the one about the sheltie puppy again."

Then she said to me, "Let's call."
"What do you mean?" I said.
"Let's call the number."
So we did.

We crept along the landing and
used the phone in Mom's new study.
We talked very quietly so Mom and Dad
wouldn't hear. The lady on the phone told
us all about the puppy. It sounded so cute.
"Ahhhhhhh," I said.
"Ohhhhhhh," said my sister.
We talked to her for a long time.
Then we crept back to bed.

The next day we were just sitting
down for lunch when the doorbell rang.
Mom went to the door.
Then she called Dad.
It was the lady from the paper.
She'd brought the puppy with her.

Mom looked embarrassed. She didn't
know what to say. Dad looked
embarrassed. He had plenty to say.

It was very bad of you to waste that lady's time. I've told you before, we are not getting a dog. No way. Not a chance. When I say no — I mean no. And I will not change my mind. Now do you understand?

One for Dad!

My sister burst out crying again.

End of Round Three.

Round Four

Not long after that, a wonderful thing happened. Well, it was wonderful for me and my sister. It wasn't very nice for Mrs. Roper, the lady who lives next door.

She had to go into the hospital to have an operation. My sister and I made get-well cards and sent them with Mom when she visited.

The WONDERFUL part of it
was that we had to look after
her dog! His name is Toby.
He is a big black labrador.
He is quite old, in dog years, and
he'd never been in a kennel.

Mrs. Roper refused to go into the
hospital until Mom promised that
we'd look after Toby.

Dad wasn't very pleased. "Dogs," he said. "I'm sick of hearing about dogs. Still, I suppose it will make *some* people happy."

We couldn't stop laughing when Mom told us.

It's okay for you, but I'm the one at home all day. I'll have to look after the old fleabag.

"Oh, Dad!" we said.
Even Mom was shocked.

"It was a joke," said Dad.

Oh, Dad!

My sister and I would have been
happy to stay all day with Toby.
In fact, each morning my sister said

she had a tummy ache

or a cold

or a sore ankle.

Dad wasn't fooled once.
He made her go to school every day.

But each night when we got home

We washed Toby's bowls, and mixed his food, and brushed his coat and took him for a walk.

When he was in a good mood,
Toby would chase a stick or a ball—
if it didn't go too far.
He never brought it back.
Toby didn't really like exercise.

Mostly Toby liked to sleep.
Sometimes he slept in his basket in
the kitchen.

Sometimes he slept in front
of the radiator.

And sometimes he slept right
against the fence, as close as he
could get to his own home.

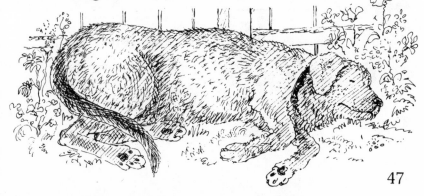

When we were at school, Toby liked
to sleep in Dad's workshop.

"He's always there under my feet,"
Dad complained.

At dinnertime each day, Dad told us
stories about what Toby had done:

how he'd chewed
the handle off
Dad's best
screwdriver,

or dug holes in
the flower bed
to bury pieces of
Dad's wood,

or eaten a whole can of wax polish
and then been sick in the sandbox.

We thought they were funny
stories. Dad didn't.

"That dog would eat anything,"
said Dad. "He must be the dumbest dog
in the world. I don't think
he's got anything
between his ears
except sawdust."

After Toby had been with
us for three weeks, it felt
like he was part of the family.
Mom saved all the scraps
for him. She made a real
fuss over him. Even Dad
stopped moaning. He didn't
exactly seem to like Toby—
he just put up with him.

But Toby certainly liked
Dad. He followed him
everywhere. When Dad
sat down in the evening,
Toby shuffled over and lay
down on Dad's feet like a
black velvet foot-warmer.

One day my sister
and I ran all the way
home from school,
to see how fast
we could do it.

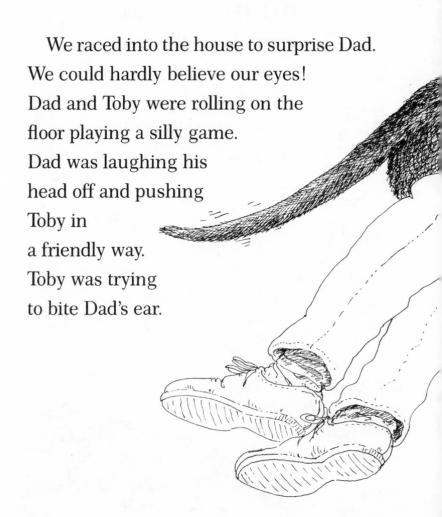

We raced into the house to surprise Dad.
We could hardly believe our eyes!
Dad and Toby were rolling on the
floor playing a silly game.
Dad was laughing his
head off and pushing
Toby in
a friendly way.
Toby was trying
to bite Dad's ear.

When Dad saw us he turned red.
He looked so embarrassed . . .
seeing us . . . seeing him . . .
playing with Toby.

I thought you said Toby was an old fleabag with no brains.

I thought you said you didn't like dogs.

You're a liar!

Dad said nothing.

What could he say?
We'd caught him.
He couldn't fool us anymore.
My sister and I stood there
grinning.

End of Round Four.

The Final Round

Soon after that, Mrs. Roper got out
of the hospital. The day she came home
we tied a big bow and a *Welcome
Home* sign around Toby's neck.
We made Mrs. Roper a cup of tea
and stayed for a while to keep her
company.

When we got home,
our own house seemed
so quiet and empty, as if
something was missing.

Something *was* missing,
and it was Toby.
Dad tried to be cheerful.

"Isn't it nice and quiet?" he said.
"No dog under our feet.

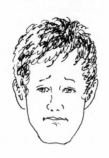

No more dog hair.
No more dog biscuits
under the cushions.
Back to normal
at last."

But nobody felt cheered up.
"Stop it," said Mom.

In bed that night my sister began to
cry. She missed Toby. Mom held her hand.
"You can still take him for walks,"
she said.

But the next day, when we visited,
Toby refused to move.

He didn't even look at us.
Now that he had Mrs. Roper back,
he wasn't going to leave her
for a minute.

The rest of the week was really boring.
When we came home from school
there was no one to play with
or take for a walk.

At dinnertime Dad had no funny stories
to tell us. In fact, nobody seemed to have
anything to say at all.

On Friday we sat at the dinner table.
I didn't feel very hungry.
My sister was making funny faces
with her salad.

Mom wasn't eating much either.

"This is a nice dinner,
isn't it?" said Dad.
No one answered.
"Did you have a good day?"
Dad asked Mom.
"All right," she said,
shrugging
her shoulders.
"Any news from school?"
Dad asked me.
"No," I said.
"Did *you* do anything exciting
today?" he asked my sister.
She didn't even answer.
She just shook her head.

Dad sat and looked at us.
"What a picture," he said. "I never
saw a more miserable family."

The Most Miserable
Family in the World

He made a really miserable face,
to get us to laugh.
We all looked miserable back.

61

Cheer up! We nearly threw a party.

Yippee!

And the very next day
we went to choose a dog.